D1123643

BMX RACERS

 WITHDRAWN

Ellen C. Labrecque

E **Enslow Publishers, Inc.**
40 Industrial Road
Box 398
Berkeley Heights, NJ 07922
USA

http://www.enslow.com

Library of Congress Cataloging-in-Publication Data
BMX racers / Ellen C. Labrecque.
    p. cm. — (Kid racers)
  Includes bibliographical references and index.
  Summary: "High interest book for reluctant readers containing action packed photos
and stories of the hottest BMX bicycles and races for kids, discussing which bikes
qualify, how they are built and raced, who the best drivers are, what to look for in
a bike, safety, good sportsmanship, and how racing activities can be a good part of
family life"—Provided by publisher.
  ISBN 978-0-7660-3484-6
  1. Bicycle motocross—Juvenile literature. I. Title.
  GV1049.3.L33 2010
  796.6'2—dc22
                                2009020785

ISBN 978-0-7660-3753-3 (paperback)

Printed in the United States of America

102009 Lake Book Manufacturing, Inc., Melrose Park, IL

10 9 8 7 6 5 4 3 2 1

To Our Readers:
We have done our best to make sure all Internet addresses in this book were active
and appropriate when we went to press. However, the author and the publisher have
no control over and assume no liability for the material available on those Internet
sites or on other Web sites they may link to. Any comments or suggestions can be sent
by e-mail to comments@enslow.com or to the address on the back cover.
    Any stunts shown in this book have been performed by experienced riders and
should not be attempted by beginners.

♻ Enslow Publishers, Inc., is committed to printing our books on recycled paper.
The paper in every book contains 10% to 30% post-consumer waste (PCW). The cover
board on the outside of each book contains 100% PCW. Our goal is to do our part to
help young people and the environment too!

Adviser: *Erma Miller, National Bicycle League, National Director of Field Operations
Union Cycliste Internationale, UCI Secretary Commissaire for Beijing 2008 Games*

Cover Photo Credit: bmxbackyard.com/Jon Larson
Interior Photo Credits: Alamy/Eric Lawton, p. 25; bergstromdesigns.com/Jason
Bergstrom, pp. 28–29; bmxbackyard.com/Jon Larson, pp.1, 23, 36, 40; Cody York
Photography, pp. 10, 11, 19, 38, 39 (top and bottom); Fotolia/Stewart Charles, p. 27;
Getty Images/Carl De Souza/AFP, p. 4; Getty Images/Phil Walter, p. 5; Getty Images, p.
8; Getty Images/Streeter Lecka, p. 24; Getty Images/Julian Finney, p. 30; Getty Images/
Matt King, p. 31; Getty Images/Heinz Kluetmeier/Sports Illustrated, p. 37; Courtesy
of Haro Bikes, p. 18; Illinois Photo/Don Northup, pp. 6, 13, 32, 35, 41; iStockphoto.
com/Peterclose, p. 7; iStockphoto.com/Isaac L. Koval, p. 26; iStockphoto.com/Nicolesy
Photography, pp. 38–39 (background); Jeff Brockmeyer, pp. 42, 43; Image courtesy
of monterey media inc./© MCMLXXI Bruce Brown Films Chad Mcqueen and Terry
Mcqueen, p. 9; Courtesy of REDLINE Bicycles, pp. 18, 20; Courtesy Sarasota Bicycle
Center/Mary McGavic, p. 14; Visions InfoLine/Jeffrey Morgan, pp. 33, 40.

Contents

Fans at the Beijing Olympic Games watch the men's BMX quarterfinals in August 2008.

LET'S RIDE!

The gate drops, and eight BMX riders take off down the 26-foot starting ramp. When they get to the bottom of the ramp, they've hit speeds of about 40 miles per hour (mph).

An Olympic Moment

It's August 22, 2008—the day of the men's and women's gold medal BMX races at the Olympic

Games in Beijing, China. BMX is making its Olympic debut. The sun is shining on the riders. They are wearing shielded helmets and brightly colored padded suits.

By the first turn, the men's race is already decided. Maris Strombergs of Latvia leads the whole time. He zooms across the finish line for first place. Mike Day and Donny Robinson of the United States win the silver and bronze medals.

Girl Speed

In the women's race, two French riders—Anne-Caroline Chausson and Laetitia le Corguille—take gold and silver. Jill Kintner of the United States wins bronze.

"We put on a great show," says Donny Robinson, "and showed everyone that the sport is really awesome."

Anne-Caroline Chausson of France celebrates her Olympic gold medal.

The Big Drop

What's it like to drop down the sloped starting ramp at a BMX race? "Imagine riding straight down the side of a three-story building," says Mike King, director of the U.S. Olympic BMX program.

BMX SPELLED OUT

BMX stands for bicycle motocross. BMX races take place on dirt tracks. Riders take big jumps and sharp turns. Pro rider Donny Robinson says a BMX race is "like riding a roller coaster."

Usually, eight riders compete in each heat, or moto. A BMX event begins with qualifying rounds. Successful riders move on to quarterfinals, semifinals, and finals.

Teenage racers compete in a moto at the 2006 BMX Midwest National Championships at Searls Park in Rockford, Illinois.

BMXers by the Thousands

Today, there are about 75,000 American BMX racers. Their ages range from four to seventy-five. Racers compete on more than five hundred tracks around the United States. The sport has four ability levels: novice (beginner), intermediate, expert, and pro. The season runs all year long—from January to December.

BMX bikes look a bit like mountain bikes, but BMX wheels are a lot smaller.

American Leaders

Two organizations run BMX races in the United States: the National Bicycle League (NBL) and the American Bicycle Association (ABA). The NBL runs races mostly on the East Coast, while the ABA operates mostly in the West. Both organizations work closely with USA Cycling, a nationwide organization for all cycling sports.

A Global Sport

BMX is popular with kids outside the United States, especially in Europe and Australia. The sport has also grown in South America. There are seventy-five national BMX federations worldwide.

3

Two boys play with their Schwinn
Sting Rays in the mid-1960s.

BMX IS BORN

BMX racing began in Southern California in the late
1970s. Here's the story.

The Sting Ray

In the early 1960s, motorcycle racing was very
popular in the United States. Schwinn, a bicycle
company, created a model called the Sting Ray
in 1963. The Sting Ray was supposed to feel like
a motorcycle. It had 20-inch wheels, which were

smaller than the wheels of other bikes. This allowed kids to turn the bike easily and to do wheelies and other simple tricks.

Copy Cats

In 1971, a motorcycle documentary called *On Any Sunday* was released. Kids watched all of their favorite motorcycles racers in action, and they began to copy the moves on their bicycles. In 1974, the first national BMX race was held. It was called the Yamaha Gold Cup, and it took place in Van Nuys, California. BMX racing was on its way!

"*Masterful... Thrills that can't be described!*"
—San Francisco Examiner

ON ANY SUNDAY

THE MOST EXCITING FILM EVER MADE ON MOTORCYCLE SPORT

Special DVD features
• Original Trailer & TV spots • Digitally Remastered
• Tribute to STEVE McQUEEN
• A Conversation with Director BRUCE BROWN

Actor Steve McQueen called *On Any Sunday* "the best thing that has ever happened to motorcycling."

BMX Time Line

1963 Schwinn creates the Sting Ray—the first BMX bike.

1971 The motorcycle movie *On Any Sunday* is released in the United States.

1974 The first national BMX race is held. *Bicycle Motocross News*, the first national magazine to cover BMX racing, publishes its first issue.

DIFFERENT WAYS TO BMX

By the mid-1970s, BMX riders were taking their new sport in different directions. Some kids in Southern California started riding in empty swimming pools. Other riders were "pulling" tricks in new skate parks.

Pulling a 360

In October 1975, the magazine *BMX Weekly* showed a picture of racer Stu Thomsen doing a 360-degree midair spin on his bike. Kids started trying Thomsen's trick. Soon, BMX riders were going freestyle.

Going Freestyle

Freestyle BMX is when riders pull tricks on their bikes. The sport is divided into five main categories: vert, street, park, dirt, and flatland. Vert riders do tricks on ramps and

Australian BMXer Corey Bohan does a Superman seat grab at the 2002 Gravity Games in Ohio.

in empty pools. Street riders do tricks on the street. Park riders do their stuff on ramps in skate parks. Dirt riders cruise over dirt jumps. Flatland riders perform on any hard surface, such as a driveway.

A dirt rider soars into the air after taking a big jump.

BMX Time Line

1984 The American Freestyle Association is formed, and freestyle BMX becomes an official sport.

1995 The first X Games (then called the Extreme Games) take place in Providence, Rhode Island.

1996 Freestyler Mat Hoffman wins his tenth vert freestyle world championship in ten years.

2001 Soaring 50 feet into the air, Hoffman sets a world record for height on a bike.

2005 *Joe Kid on a Sting-Ray* is released. This documentary tells the story of BMX.

2008 BMX makes its Olympic debut at the Summer Games in Beijing, China.

11

START WITH THE BASICS

Before you start racing, you need to find the right bike. You can use most bicycles with 20-to-24-inch wheels. A 20-inch is a standard BMX bike. A 24-inch bike is known as a cruiser. BMXers don't use equipment that sticks out, such as kickstands, chain guards, and reflectors.

Find a Track

Next, hit the Internet and find a track near you. If you live on the East Coast, check out the National Bicycle League (NBL) Web site. For tracks in the Midwest or on the West Coast, check the American Bicycle Association (ABA). Once you find the track, ask about special days for first-time riders to practice. Your first day at a BMX track should not be for a race.

Take a Friend

When you take your first ride at a track, go with an experienced friend or a member of the track

12

staff. Lots of kids learn from older friends or siblings. Eleven-year-old Kelsey Van Ogle of Auburn, Washington, learned to ride from her older brother, fifteen-year-old Lain. "Kelsey now rides with straight power because of her bro's guidance," says Greg Leasure of the American Bicycle Association.

Get a Membership

Are you ready to race? Sign up for an NBL or ABA membership. (This usually costs about forty-five dollars a year.) The membership lets you participate in races and practice on the organization's tracks. You will also receive a number plate for your bike and a membership license for you to use when you register for events.

When you find a track, you will probably find a friendly group of racers. Their support will help you concentrate on your riding.

6

Measure the top tube to find the right size BMX bike for you.

FINDING A BIKE

Are you ready to find the right BMX bike for you? First, decide what you want to do on your bike. There are four kinds of BMX bikes: racing, dirt jumping, freestyle (vert, street, and park), and flatland.

Know Your Purpose

If you want to race, buy a bike that is lightweight and easy to pedal fast. If you plan to do dirt jumping or freestyle moves, get a heavier bike. The stronger the bike, the better it will handle all the tricks you pull.

The Right Fit

Next, decide how big the bike should be. Ask the experts at the bike store for help. They'll be able to find the right fit for you. Most BMX frames are 19 to 22 inches long. Picking out a bike is like trying on new pants. You may have to "try on" a few bikes until you find just the right one.

Looking for a Deal

BMX bikes can be expensive. Greg Leasure of the American Bicycle Association says beginners can get a good bike for less than 250 dollars. You can find great deals on used bikes on the Internet. Also, most bike stores sell used bikes or last year's models at good prices.

What to Look for in a Bike

Greg Leasure, track director of the ABA, offers these tips on how to shop for a bike:

1. *Find a bike that is the right fit for you.* Don't choose style over comfort.

2. *Buy a bike that is already assembled.* It's less expensive and safer than buying parts and putting them together yourself.

3. *Don't spend money on accessories such as pegs and kickstands.* They aren't allowed in races anyway.

THE RACING BIKE

A racing bike is best for dirt track racing and going fast for short distances off-road. Racing bikes don't have accessories such as kickstands, reflectors, or even front brakes. The less "stuff" on the bike, the safer it is to race, and the faster you will go. Some of the top brands of racing bikes for kids and pros are Redline, Haro, Mongoose, and GT.

A 2009 Redline Flight Expert

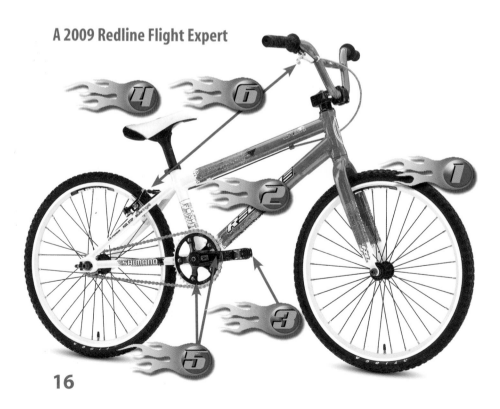

1. *Wheels*—The tires are extra-knobby to provide a good grip on dirt tracks. The front tire has no brake—it is not necessary for racing. The wheels usually have thirty-two spokes.

2. *Frame*—Most racers like their bike as light as possible, because it goes faster that way. The lighter the frame, the more expensive the bike will be. The lightest frames are made of aluminum, which does not rust.

3. *Pedals*—Sharp teeth on the pedals help provide the best grip.

4. *Seat*—The seat moves up and down, so the bike can grow as you grow.

5. *Cranks and Chainwheels*—These parts send your "pedal power" to the wheels. The taller you are, the longer the crank arm will need to be.

6. *Brakes*—Racing bikes have only a rear brake. A pull grip on the handlebar gives you the best stopping power.

THE DIRT-JUMPING BIKE

Dirt-jumping bikes are best for riding around town, jumping over dirt hills, and riding on trails. Some of the best dirt-jumping brands are Intense BMX, Haro, and Mirra.

Shown here is Haro's dirt-jumping model Forum Counterpart Lite.

1. *Wheels*—These tires have the heaviest treads of all BMX bikes. They provide the ultimate grip while jumping and landing on dirt hills. Like the racing bike, the front tire of a dirt jumper has no brake.

2. *Frame*—The frame should be sturdy to last through plenty of pounding from jumps.

3. *Brakes*—Dirt-jumping bikes have rear brakes called U-brakes. These brakes are a bit gentler than racing bike brakes, so that dirt jumpers can do certain tricks.

4. *Seat*—The seat is large and cushioned. This helps soften the blow on landings.

Average Bike Weights

BMX freestyle bike:
26 pounds and above

BMX racing bike:
20 to 23 pounds

Professional road-racing bike:
15 pounds

Freestyle rider Jamie Bestwick pulls a downside tailwhip.

19

FREESTYLE AND FLATLAND BIKES

Freestyle and flatland bikes are almost the same. The main difference is that flatland bikes have smaller frames. Both types of bikes are used for doing highly technical tricks on smooth surfaces. Freestyle bikes are often used for pulling stunts in skate parks. Some of the best freestyle and flatland brands are Mirra, Haro, Mongoose, and Redline.

A 2009 Redline RL 3.2

1. **Wheels**—The tires have fairly smooth treads. They are designed for pavement, which is easy to grip. Each wheel has two pegs. These are used for tricks.

2. **Handlebars**—The handlebars rise steeply to give riders more room for tricks. The front brake cable is usually run through a detangler or gyro.

3. **Gyro**—The gyro allows the handlebars to spin all the way around without tangling up the cable.

4. **Frame**—The frame is sturdy and thick. It needs to be durable enough for all kinds of tricks. Freestyle bikes are much heavier than racing bikes.

5. **Seat**—The seat is usually made of hard plastic. Riders often stand on their seats when pulling certain tricks.

6. **Front and rear brakes**—Unlike other BMX bikes, freestyle and flatland bikes have brakes on both tires. This helps the rider perform tricks that require immediate stops.

SAFETY GEAR

BMX riding is a blast, but it can be dangerous. With a little bit of equipment, you'll be as safe as possible. Wear your safety gear every single time you hop on your bike.

Helmet

Your helmet is the most important part of your safety gear. Why? A lot of young riders find their head moves around quite a bit when they ride. Nine-year-old Madison Martinez of Valencia, California, is even known for her bobble-head style of racing!

For racing, helmets should have a full face guard. For freestyle riding, a skate helmet should protect you from injury—but advanced freestyle riders use helmets with face guards as well. Make sure your helmet is approved by the U.S. Consumer Product Safety Commission (CPSC).

"Spend the extra money on a certified helmet," says Dave Mirra, a legendary pro BMX freestyle rider. "This is an area where you don't want to save money."

Pads

Both racers and freestylers wear a basic set of skate pads that cover their knees and elbows. Don't be fooled by pro freestylers who look like they aren't wearing pads. Their style is to wear the pads underneath their pants. Many top pros wear shin and ankle guards as well.

Gloves

Most BMX riders wear gloves. Biking gloves help prevent blisters and make sure your hands don't slip off the handlebars. Your biking gloves should fit tightly.

Shoes

BMXers must wear closed-toe shoes. Make sure the bottoms have good treads on them so they don't slip off the pedals.

This BMX rider is geared up for a safe ride, all the way from his helmet down to his sturdy shoes.

Crashes happen even in professional BMX races. Here, riders take a spill in a turn at the Beijing Olympic finals.

RIDE SMART, RIDE SAFE

Wearing the right equipment is only part of being a safe BMXer. You also need to *ride* safely. Remember, don't ride above your ability level—especially in freestyle. Start with the easier tricks. It takes a long time and a lot of practice to perform the hard tricks successfully.

Make Room for Your Bike

Stay aware of your surroundings as well as other riders. While racing, don't try to dart through the pack when there isn't a big enough opening. If you're riding in a skate park, make sure all ramps are clear before you take off.

Be smart about where you ride. Do not perform tricks in parking lots and on the street. These are dangerous and unacceptable places to ride. And remember, *always* wear your safety gear, especially your helmet.

These kid racers are riding a bit too close together. They need more space around their bikes.

"I've had a lot of injuries that could have been prevented if I'd been wearing safety gear," says BMX freestyler Dave Mirra. "Now, I feel naked without [my gear]."

Bike Checks

Before every ride, do a quick bike check. Make sure of these things:

✔ your brakes are working
✔ all bolts and screws are tight
✔ your seat is secure
✔ your tires have the right amount of air

WHERE TO RIDE

Sometimes BMX riders just want to step outside, jump on their bikes, and go for a ride. There is no reason you can't do this. You just have to be smart about riding around town.

On Side Streets—Remember to obey all traffic signs and rules. Save your tricks and jumps for the track. Watch closely for people crossing the street or playing games.

Backyards—Are you looking for bumps and dirt? Try riding around your backyard (with an

North America's Top Five Bike-Friendly Cities

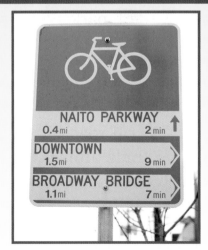

NAITO PARKWAY
0.4 mi   2 min

DOWNTOWN
1.5 mi   9 min

BROADWAY BRIDGE
1.1 mi   7 min

I. Portland, Oregon
2. Boulder, Colorado
3. San Diego, California
4. Montreal, Canada
5. Davis, California

Source: ForbesTraveler.com

The city of Portland, Oregon, has lots of biker-friendly signs.

This BMXer has a choice of two riding surfaces. He can ride on the grass or try out some dirt jumps.

adult's approval, of course). You can even set up your own racetrack.

Skate Parks—Skate parks are safe places for riders to practice tricks. However, many of them do not allow bikes. Before showing up on your bike, find out if your local skate park allows riders. Some parks have certain hours when only bikers are allowed.

Trails—Your local park probably has trails where you can take your bike off road. It can even be exciting to hit the trails after a big rainfall. Bikes and mud are a fun combination!

TRACK POWER

Are you ready to hit a track? Tracks can be anywhere from 900 to 1,200 feet long. Usually, there are three turns and four straightaways.

Tom Sawyer State Park
One of the biggest and best tracks in the United States is in E. P. "Tom" Sawyer State Park in Louisville, Kentucky. It hosts the National BMX Grand Championships every year on Labor Day weekend. The track is open for practicing when there isn't a race going on.

Track Breakdown

Most tracks, like the one in Kentucky, include the same features.

Start hill: usually about a 10-foot-long sloped hill. Riders try to pick up the most speed here.

Speed jumps: rounded hills that riders can cruise or jump over. Riders try not to jump too high, so they won't lose speed in the air.

Sweeper: a flat bend without a bank

Table top: a basic jump with a flat middle section

Berms: banked turns. Riders can wipe out on berms if they aren't careful.

Rhythm section: a line of small jumps

Whoops: steep speed jumps set in pairs

29

STAR TRACKS

The BMX track built for the 2008 Olympics was the most challenging track ever designed. In addition to the 26-foot starting ramp, it had a 10-foot dirt jump. On the men's course, riders took a 35-foot jump over the women's course!

"When we first saw the track in China, it made our jaws drop because it was so much bigger than the regular Supercross tracks," said American rider Donny Robinson, who won a bronze medal at the 2008 games.

The Laoshan BMX track was built for the 2008 Olympic Games in China. The stands seat four thousand fans.

Carbon Copy

Not to be outdone, the U.S. team built almost the exact same track for riders to train on at the U.S. Olympic Training Center in Chula Vista, California. With the help of the best engineers in the world, the U.S. track was built in three months. It cost about $450,000.

With the Olympics long past, what's next for the U.S. track? It will be redesigned to match the 2012 Olympic track in London, England.

In His Backyard

BMX rider Luke Madill of Sydney, Australia, went to extremes to chase gold at the 2008 Olympics. He built an exact replica of the Olympic track . . . in his backyard!

At first, Madill tried to keep the track secret. But word soon leaked out, and riders asked if they could practice on it.

Madill's personal track didn't help as much as he hoped. At the Olympics, he was knocked out in the quarterfinals.

You can feel the excitement when BMX riders line up at the starting gate.

RACE DAY

Race day at the track feels like a big party. Families and friends are there to cheer on the riders. Fans set up picnics and tents around the track. Music blares from the loudspeakers. Volunteers and staff members are also milling around. They will help answer any questions you might have.

Start with Signup

On race day, arrive early so you can register and take some practice runs. Once you have finished practicing, check out the moto board. On the board you'll find your race number and gate lane for each race. Write these numbers down on your hand or a piece of paper.

Keep Your Ears Open

Listen to the announcer on the loudspeaker. The announcer will tell you when your races are coming up. Right before the race, officials will check out your bike to make sure it is safe.

And You're On!

Once it is race time, relax and have fun. Listen for the shouting and clapping as you come around the turns. Your family and friends will all be cheering for you!

Fans watch a race from the sidelines in Flemington, New Jersey.

BE A WINNER

Once you've mastered the basics of BMX, it's time to develop a racing strategy. The first rule is simple: practice, practice, practice! Try to hit as many different tracks as possible. The more hills and jumps you ride, the better you'll become. Also, invite friends along when you ride. The more riders, the more fun!

Learn from a Pro

Some kid riders even train with the pros. Ten-year-old Vaughn Herrick, who is known for his fearless style, won the 2008 national championship in his age division. Vaughn practices with U.S. Olympian Kyle Bennett. They are both from the same hometown—Conroe, Texas.

The Best Start

Once you are comfortable on the track, learn to balance at the starting gate with both feet on the pedals. This gives you a much faster start. Then go as fast as you can out of the gate and try to get the holeshot, or first position. This puts you ahead of the pack and helps you avoid getting in a tangle with other bikers.

Rider 83 has the holeshot out of the starting gate. His best strategy is to keep the same position during the whole race.

Once you are in front, hold your position. Don't try to hit other riders, but don't let them knock you around either. When you hit jumps, stay low. Remember, it is called BMX racing. You're going for speed, not for major air.

Riding the Turns

Finally, try to stay on the outside of other riders on turns. On the outside line, you can see what everybody else is doing. This puts you in charge of the race. Keep pedaling all the way through the finish line. Many riders slow down, only to have another rider pass them for the win!

BEST OF THE BEST

Looking for some pros and fellow kid riders to look up to? Here are just a few of the big names in BMX.

Hunter Stephens competes in a qualifying race in Richmond, Virginia, in May 2009.

Hunter Stephens
Fredericksburg, Virginia

2008 ten-year-old NBL rookie champion

Stephens did not get on a bike until he was eight years old. But once he started riding BMX and got tips from pro riders, he took off.

Felicia Stancil
Lake Villa, Illinois

2004, 2005, and 2007 world champion

Felicia "Fly-N" Stancil, a teenage BMX rider, has "mad" skills. She rides hard and gets big air. If she keeps up this pace, Stancil could be good enough to ride in the 2012 Olympics.

Jill Kintner, Seattle, Washington
2008 Olympic bronze medalist

Kintner retired from BMX racing in 2002 at the top of her game. She had just won the 2002 world championship and had over seventy career wins. Soon after her retirement, she decided to become a professional mountaincross racer. On her mountain bike, she won three world champion titles (2005, 2006, and 2007). Then she heard BMX was going to be an Olympic sport. She couldn't resist returning to her first love. In Beijing, Kintner captured a bronze medal.

Mike Day, Chula Vista, California
2008 Olympic silver medallist

Mike Day has a saying that he uses to calm himself before every race: "Relax. Ready. Holeshot." Getting the holeshot means being the first rider to get to the first turn of the race. At the Olympics, Day just barely missed gold, but his silver made him proud.

Left to right: BMX stars Kyle Bennett, Mike Day, and Jill Kintner pose at the U.S. Olympic Team trials in Chula Vista, California.

IT'S TRICKY

If you prefer freestyle to racing, here are some tricks to try. Remember, always wear safety equipment. And don't try any trick unless you feel completely comfortable. Know your limits.

Bunny Hop

This is an aerial move on a bike. A lot of riders do bunny hops over curbs. You roll forward, lean back, and pull up on the handlebars. Next, lift your knees to help the back wheel lift off the ground. Once in the air, level the tires so you come back down evenly.

A rider completes a bunny hop. He seems to rest lightly on a piece of tape in midair!

Bar Spin

Practice a bar spin on the ground first. You should start with your left hand backward on the grip and your right hand forward. While riding along, spin the handlebars clockwise 180 degrees. Once you have mastered this, try spinning the handlebars 360 degrees (all the way around) on flat ground.

In a bar spin, the rider turns his handlebars all the way around.

Can Can

You need to get some air to do this trick. Launch yourself off a ramp, and kick your left or right foot over to the opposite side of the bike. The other foot stays on the pedal.

A more advanced trick is the no-footed can can. In this trick, you remove both feet from the pedals.

A no-footed can can

39

Families cheer on their favorite racers at the NBL Keystone Nationals, held in Pottstown, Pennsylvania.

FAMILY FUN

What's the best part of BMX? The races? The tricks? The dirt? All these things are fabulous. But what makes BMX truly special is that it is a family affair. Nobody is left on the sidelines! After all, a racer's age can be anywhere from four to seventy-five.

"Mom and dad are yelling at their kid to pedal," says Greg Leasure of the American Bicycle Association. "Then, the kid can turn it around and yell at his mom or dad to pedal harder too."

Loving the Noise

With all this yelling and cheering, BMX races are loud. Gates crash with a bang, the announcers chatter nonstop, and music blares from the loudspeakers. All this noise only adds to the fun!

On the Road

Many times, families plan their vacations around the biggest BMX races of the year. They travel with campers and tents and stay at or near the racetracks. Families pack plenty of food to make sure that everybody stays fueled throughout the day.

After their own events, kid racers often get to cheer for their siblings or parents.

CAMP WOODWARD

Way out in the woods of central Pennsylvania is a BMX paradise. Actually, it is a paradise for most action sports. It is called Camp Woodward, and it has 80 acres of ramps, street courses, dirt jumps, and bowl complexes for action sports athletes. It also has 175,000 square feet of indoor facilities, so athletes can train there all year long. Camp Woodward also has locations in California, Wisconsin, and Colorado.

Kids at Woodward

Camp Woodward isn't just for the pros. From June to August, Woodward hosts kids from ages seven to eighteen. They come from

Kids at Camp Woodward compete in a high-jump contest.

Some of the instructors at Camp Woodward are racing pros, such as Will Greathouse (far left).

all over the country. Woodward even sets up foam pits for young campers. This allows BMX riders to try new tricks without getting injured.

BMX Speak

brain bucket—a helmet
kicker—a jump ramp
potato chip—a bent bicycle wheel
Superman—a trick where a rider poses in a flying motion during a jump

For the Pros, Too

"Woodward has boosted bike stunt so much," says Kevin Robinson, a professional BMX vert rider. "Pros come from all over the world to use this facility."

GLOSSARY

accessories—Extra parts that go with something. For example, a kickstand is an extra part that comes with a bike.

aerial—Happening in midair.

assembled—Put together, with all parts in place.

cruiser bicycles—Standard bicycles sold in most bike or toy stores. They usually have heavy-duty frames and at least a 24-inch wheel.

debut—A first public appearance.

documentary—A movie about real people, places, and events.

federations—Groups of smaller organizations with a similar purpose.

frame—The main part of a bike that connects the wheels and all other parts.

gyro (detangler)—A bike part that allows the handlebars to spin all the way around without tangling up the brake cable.

holeshot—The first rider out of the starting gate.

intermediate—A person who is fairly good at something; neither a beginner nor an expert.

moto—A heat, or round of a race, at a BMX event.

pegs—Parts of a freestyle bike that screw on where the tire is mounted to the frame. They are the size and shape of a roll of quarters. They can be screwed onto the back or front wheel. Pegs are used for tricks.

pull—To do a trick.

skate parks—Parks built for skateboarders, inline skaters, and BMX bikers to ride and develop their technique. The parks are filled with ramps and jumps.

straightaways—Long, straight sections of a track or road.

top tube—The part of a bicycle frame that stretches across the top of the bike from the seat to the back wheel.

treads—The parts of a bicycle tire that grip the road.

vert—An extreme sport held on a U-shaped ramp that allows athletes to move up and down (vertically).

FURTHER READING

Books

David, Jack. *BMX Racing*. Danbury, Connecticut: Children's Press, 2007.

Higgins, Matt. *Insiders Guide to Action Sports*. New York: Scholastic, 2006.

Mahaney, Ian F. *Dave Mirra: BMX Champion*. New York: Rosen Pub. Group, 2005.

McClellan, Ray. *BMX Freestyle*. New York: Bellwether Media, 2008.

Weil, Ann. *BMX Racing*. Mankato, Minn.: Capstone Press, 2005.

Web Sites

American Bicycle Association—*One of two governing bodies for the sport of BMX*
<www.ababmx.com>

Camp Woodward—*Read all about the action sports camp*
<www.campwoodward.com>

National Bicycle League—*The other governing body for BMX in the United States*
<www.nbl.org>

INDEX